Hugg 'n' Bugg

Finding Home

Ian Brown & Eoin Clarke

Look very hard. Can you see
Little Bugg, the mountain flea?
He's not really hiding, he's just so small,
Here where the mountains are tallest of all.

2

3

Most who live here don't mind the cold,
But this flea is different, if truth be told.

4

He doesn't like ice. He doesn't like snow.
He shivers and quivers and hops to and fro.

5

So he sets off in search of somewhere warm
To shelter himself from the snowy storm.

He has chattering teeth and knocking knees
And now and again a very loud sneeze.

He lives, for a while, under a rock,
In the well-worn folds of a long-lost sock.
But the rock and the sock
don't really suit,

Nor for that matter
does a smelly old
boot.

He says goodbye and hops up on
A passing leopard, known as Ron.

But Ron the leopard
moves too fast,
And all Bugg feels is
an icy blast.

Next, a goat and some shaggy yaks
Make space for Bugg upon their
backs.

Alas, that too won't do the trick,
And he's soon flicked off by a
slobbery lick.

Bugg still has itchy feet to roam
In search of the perfect, comfy home,
So he scales the mountain, cold and high,
Looking for somewhere warm and dry.

He closes his eyes for one last leap...
And lands in something soft and deep.
"This certainly feels a nice place to be.
But just where am I?" asks Bugg the flea.

He has found the hairiest beast of all,
A snowman that's furry and extremely tall.
Some men of science call him Yeti.
They don't let on he has hair like spaghetti.

He's the Abominable Snowman - or 'Hugg' to the knowing -
He has so much dandruff, when he walks it starts snowing.

18

Hugg can't say his own full name,
To him, the words all sound the same.
"I'm Bummy Nubble Snowman," he says with glee.
No one ever dares to disagree.

"Why have I not
seen you here before?"
Bugg asks. "You're so huge
and hard to ignore."

"Because I do not want to be found.
That's why I live up on the highest ground.
I always look such a terrible sight,
I give any visitors an awful fright."

"You don't scare me," says Bugg, acting bold.
"I'm only shaking because I'm still a bit cold.
Let me live here in your nice warm hair,
And I will look after you. I'll take good care."

Hugg has fur all over the place,
Whiskers in his ears and over his face.
Hair covers his eyes and sprouts from his nose.
He even has ten of the hairiest toes.

For Bugg, the top of Hugg's giant head
Is by far the best spot to make his bed.

Plenty of space for a flea to choose
Which way to admire the spectacular views,

And just a short hop for some tasty snacks
Made out of Hugg's own gooey earwax.

Down on Hugg's chin Bugg can really tuck in.

There's so much to choose from, where to begin?

Dried bits of egg and stuff that's gone green,

All picked from Hugg's fur, so it's kept nice and clean.

He works his way down to the great furry belly,

And even dares go where things get a bit smelly.

25

26

Before his flea came to stay,
Hugg would be alone all day.

But now they've both found
their ideal chums —
While Hugg keeps Bugg warm,
The flea eats his crumbs,

All the while taking
the greatest care
Of his best friend's
long and shaggy hair.

28

A very snug bug
And his smart living rug.
Way up high where not many have been,
Hugg looks so neat,
From his top to his feet,
That he no longer fears being seen.

Now plenty of visitors
travel for miles,
To see Hugg showing off
his brand-new hairstyles.

Ian Brown

Ian is a former journalist, turned television writer and producer. After a spell on local and national newspapers, a thirty-year career in television has included news, documentaries, commercials, comedy and entertainment shows. He has written or produced for a host of household names, picking up several awards along the way. He's also often heard on radio talking about television. Writing for children has been a long-held dream. Ian shares his home with, among others, wife Millie, two cats and a tortoise called Albert, who inspired Ian's first series of picture books from Graffeg.

Eoin Clarke

Eoin qualified with a BA in Graphic Design from Middlesex University and an MA in Animation from the Royal College of Art. He has worked for thirty years in the animation industry as a director, animator, designer and storyboard artist. He has directed films, commercials, documentaries and title sequences and has picked up thirty awards as a director, working on projects for, among others, the BBC, Channel 4 and the British Film Institute. Eoin is also the illustrator for the Albert the Tortoise series.

Also in this series:

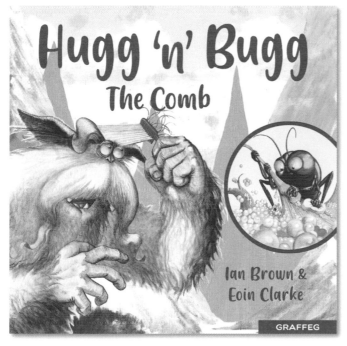

Hugg 'n' Bugg: The Comb
ISBN 9781802583069

Other books by Ian Brown and Eoin Clarke:

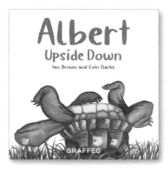

Albert Upside Down
ISBN 9701913634162

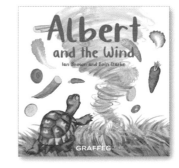

Albert and the Wind
ISBN 9781913733445

Albert Supersize
ISBN 9781802580167

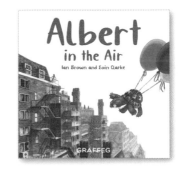

Albert in the Air
ISBN 9781802580174

Hugg 'n' Bugg: Finding Home
Published in Great Britain in 2022 by Graffeg Limited.

ISBN 9781802582000

Written by Ian Brown copyright © 2022.
Illustrated by Eoin Clarke copyright © 2022.
Designed and produced by Graffeg Limited
copyright © 2022.

Graffeg Limited, 15 Neptune Court, Vanguard Way, Cardiff,
CF24 5PJ, Wales, UK. Tel: +44(0)1554 824000.
sales@graffeg.com www.graffeg.com

The publisher acknowledges the financial support of the
Books Council of Wales. www.gwales.com

Teaching Resources: www.graffeg.com/pages/teachers-resources

1 2 3 4 5 6 7 8 9

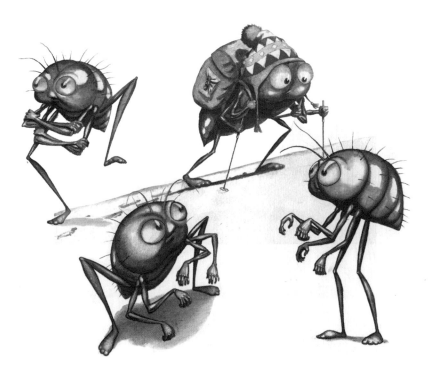

36